# The Winter
# Princess

# ★ Also by ★
# Debbie Dadey

## MERMAID TALES

BOOK 1: *TROUBLE AT TRIDENT ACADEMY*

BOOK 2: *BATTLE OF THE BEST FRIENDS*

BOOK 3: *A WHALE OF A TALE*

BOOK 4: *DANGER IN THE DEEP BLUE SEA*

BOOK 5: *THE LOST PRINCESS*

BOOK 6: *THE SECRET SEA HORSE*

BOOK 7: *DREAM OF THE BLUE TURTLE*

BOOK 8: *TREASURE IN TRIDENT CITY*

BOOK 9: *A ROYAL TEA*

BOOK 10: *A TALE OF TWO SISTERS*

BOOK 11: *THE POLAR BEAR EXPRESS*

BOOK 12: *WISH UPON A STARFISH*

BOOK 13: *THE CROOK AND THE CROWN*

BOOK 14: *TWIST AND SHOUT*

BOOK 15: *BOOKS VS. LOOKS*

BOOK 16: *FLOWER GIRL DREAMS*

BOOK 17: *READY, SET, GOAL!*

BOOK 18: *FAIRY CHASE*

BOOK 19: *THE NARWHAL PROBLEM*

## Coming Soon

BOOK 21: *SLEEPOVER AT THE HAUNTED MUSEUM*

# Mermaid Tales

*★Debbie Dadey★*

Illustrated by
Tatevik Avakyan

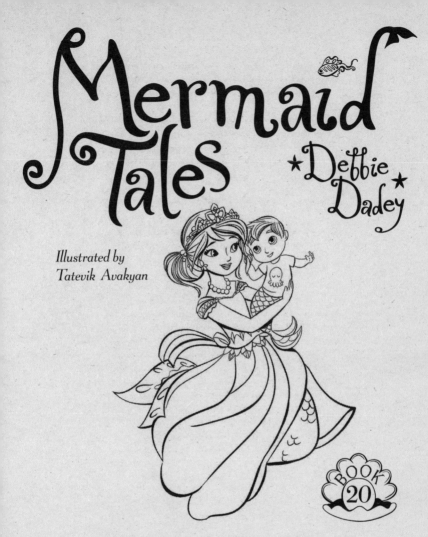

BOOK 20

## The Winter Princess

**ALADDIN**

NEW YORK   LONDON   TORONTO   SYDNEY   NEW DELHI

## ALADDIN

An imprint of Simon & Schuster Children's Publishing Division

1230 Avenue of the Americas, New York, New York 10020

First Aladdin paperback edition June 2020

Text copyright © 2020 by Debbie Dadey

Illustrations copyright © 2020 by Tatevik Avakyan

Also available in an Aladdin hardcover edition.

All rights reserved, including the right of reproduction in whole or in part in any form.

ALADDIN and related logo are registered trademarks of Simon & Schuster, Inc.

For information about special discounts for bulk purchases, please contact Simon & Schuster

Special Sales at 1-866-506-1949 or business@simonandschuster.com.

The Simon & Schuster Speakers Bureau can bring authors to your live event.

For more information or to book an event contact the Simon & Schuster Speakers Bureau

at 1-866-248-3049 or visit our website at www.simonspeakers.com.

Cover designed by Tiara Iandiorio

Interior designed by Mike Rosamilia

The text of this book was set in Belucian Book.

Manufactured in the United States of America 0520 OFF

2 4 6 8 10 9 7 5 3 1

Library of Congress Control Number 2019934416

ISBN 978-1-4814-8718-4 (hc)

ISBN 978-1-4814-8717-7 (pbk)

ISBN 978-1-4814-8719-1 (eBook)

*To my son Alex, who made*

*our family complete.*

*And to great young readers*

*Alice, Lillian, and Emma.*

# Contents

1   GREAT NEWS?     1

2   BOOM. BOOM. BOOM.     8

3   BROTHERS     15

4   PEARL'S NEWS     20

5   SHOCKED     27

6   CRYING BABIES

    AND KILLER WHALES     34

7   PERFECT DRESS     40

8   SLIME TIME     46

9   PEOPLE MUSEUM     52

10   THE MOST IMPORTANT THING     58

11   DIAMOND DRESS     64

12   GOOD ADVICE     71

    CLASS REPORTS     77

    THE MERMAID TALES SONG     82

    AUTHOR'S NOTE     84

    GLOSSARY     86

# Great News?

**P**EARL SWAMP COULDN'T believe her luck. Out of all the third graders at Trident Academy, her name had been drawn to be the princess at this year's Winter Festival! If it had been a merboy, they would have had a winter prince. Every year Trident City celebrated the end of the coldest waters with a huge party at the People Museum. All the money raised went to help families in need.

Pearl had dreamed all her life of being the winter princess! It was the most exciting thing to ever happen to her. She would wear a fancy dress, give the welcome speech, and be the official ambassador for her school. She couldn't wait to share the news with her parents.

Pearl zipped through MerPark, around a glass squid, and dashed inside the large pink shell she shared with her parents. "Mom!"

Her mother popped out of her home office and smiled. "Pearl! I've been waiting for you."

"I have great news," they both said at the same time.

Pearl was surprised. Did her mother already know?

"What's your news?" her mother asked.

"You can go first," Pearl said.

Her mother clapped her hands. "You are not going to believe it! You're getting a baby brother!"

Pearl hadn't expected that at all. She opened her mouth. She closed her mouth. Finally, she squeaked, "A baby?"

"Yes," squealed her mother. "Isn't it exciting? We're adopting a little merboy."

"A merboy?" Pearl muttered. "Why a merboy?"

Mrs. Swamp giggled like a young child. "Well, we already have a lovely daughter. Don't you think a merboy will be nice?"

Pearl frowned. A baby mergirl might have been fun. She could have dressed it in frilly dresses and had tea parties. But she wasn't so sure about a merboy.

"Does Daddy know about this?"

Her mother smiled. "Well, of course. This is something we've planned for a long time."

Her parents had talked to her about adopting a baby, but that had been a while ago. Pearl thought they had forgotten about the whole thing. Why in the ocean did they want a baby? Wasn't she enough for them?

"Pearl?"

Pearl wanted to stomp her gold fins and tell her parents to forget about a baby. But her mother looked so hopeful and happy, Pearl just couldn't. Instead she fibbed, "I can't wait."

Her mother gave her a hug. "I've dreamed of giving our new baby a good home. Our family will be complete."

Pearl thought it had been pretty perfect with just the three of them, but she didn't say so.

"Oh, that reminds me," her mother said. "I'm going to clean out the craft room for the baby's bedroom."

"What?" Pearl couldn't believe her ears. Pearl and her mother loved their hobby room. It was filled with colorful shells, beads, and ribbons. They'd had many fin-tastic times making all sorts of fun creations. And now her mom was going to get rid of it all? "But where will we do our projects?"

"Don't worry," Mrs. Swamp said. "Most merpeople don't have a craft room and they do just fine. It's too bad that Anna is visiting her daughter this month. I could use her help."

Pearl frowned. Losing her craft room did not sound fine at all. She wished Anna, their maid, wasn't out of town too. Anna was more like a second mother to Pearl. And right now, Pearl really needed to talk to her.

Mrs. Swamp floated up their curving marble staircase. She disappeared around the corner before Pearl realized her mother had forgotten to ask about Pearl's good news!

## Boom. Boom. Boom.

**T**HE NEXT MORNING PEARL'S friend, Wanda, met her at the doorway of their classroom. "I bet your mom was thrilled that you're going to be the winter princess."

Pearl nodded. She was too upset to tell Wanda what had really happened. Her parents had talked nonstop all evening about getting things ready for the baby. Pearl had gone to bed early with a terrible headache. In fact, her head still ached all during spelling and math lessons.

Pearl groaned when she realized it was time for music class. The last thing she wanted was noisy instruments, but she didn't have much choice. Unfortunately, Mr. Pebble, the music teacher, assigned her the shark-skin drum.

"Let's work on getting the beat right," Mr. Pebble said as he adjusted his bow tie.

*Boom. Boom. Boom.* Pearl tried to keep up with the other instruments. Wanda was playing a guitarfish, while a thin cornet-fish twisted around Shelly. Echo was doing

a decent job with a banjo ray. Adam blew into conch shell as Rocky tapped a black drum fish. Only Kiki's music from the trumpet fish sounded pretty. Everything else was making Pearl's headache much worse!

*Boom. Boom. Boom.* Pearl tried not to think about the new baby. She tried not to think about her parents ignoring her. But suddenly between her headache and her heartache she couldn't stand it anymore. Right in the middle of music class she started crying.

Mr. Pebble rubbed his hands over his slicked-back hair. "Miss Swamp, is something amiss?"

Pearl was embarrassed when everyone

stopped playing and looked at her. She couldn't help blurting out, "My parents are adopting a baby merboy!"

Wanda smiled and touched Pearl on the shoulder. "That's wonderful news."

"Cool," Rocky said. "I'm adopted."

Pearl frowned at Wanda and Rocky. "You don't understand!" Pearl pushed her drum away and swam out of the room.

Pearl soared into the library. It was her favorite place in the school and thankfully the quietest. Even Miss Scylla, the librarian, didn't seem to be in the darkened space.

Pearl stared up at the mother-of-pearl domed ceiling and the sleeping mauve stinger jellyfish on the chandeliers. She sat and laid her head on one of the marble tables. After a few minutes she felt a bit calmer.

"Pearl?" Kiki said softly. "Would you like some company?"

Pearl wasn't sure what she wanted. But Kiki was one of the nicest mergirls in her class, so she lifted her head and nodded.

"It's kind of scary to get a little brother," Kiki said.

"Do you have a brother?" Pearl asked. She couldn't remember if Kiki had told her about her family.

Kiki smiled. "I have seventeen. . . ."

"Seventeen!" Pearl shouted, then looked around to make sure Miss Scylla wasn't about.

Kiki laughed. "Yes, but only one little brother. My mom said I was a little grumpy at first when Yuta came along."

Pearl put a hand on Kiki's arm. "Tell me the truth. Is it terrible?"

# Brothers

**M**Y BROTHERS ARE LOTS of fun," Kiki said with a smile. "Except when they are playing pranks on me. One time they actually filled my bed with sea slugs."

"That's horrible," Pearl said.

Kiki shrugged. "We play lots of games together."

Pearl thought that sounded rather nice. After all, her parents weren't always interested in playing with her in the evenings.

Kiki laughed. "Sometimes they get really excited. Between the yelling and screaming, I can't hear myself think!"

"That doesn't sound good." Pearl frowned. "I'm going to tell my parents to make sure we have a quiet baby."

Pearl heard a giggle as her friend Wanda swam into the library. "There's no such thing as a quiet baby."

"How do you know?" Pearl asked.

"Before I left to come to Trident

Academy, my little sister, Emelia, was born," Wanda explained. "Sometimes she cried half the night." Wanda lived in the school's dormitory, along with Kiki. Their homes were too far away to go back to at night.

"Why would someone want a baby if it cries all the time?" Pearl couldn't understand why her parents would even consider such craziness.

"They aren't little forever," Kiki told her. "I did like telling my little brother stories, and he laughed when I made silly faces."

"I loved it when Emelia squeezed my finger and blew bubbles," Wanda said.

"Babies can be really cute," Kiki admitted.

Wanda nodded. "Except when they are spitting up."

"And when you have to change poopy diapers," Kiki added.

"Poopy diapers!" Pearl shrieked.

Wanda held her nose. "They smell terrible!"

Pearl soared away from the table as the conch bell sounded to start lunchtime. "I don't want to change poopy diapers or get spit up on. And I really don't want to hear a baby crying all night long."

Wanda shrugged. "There's not much you can do about it. Babies are just that way."

"That doesn't mean I have to like it," Pearl told the mergirls.

"It's not that bad," Kiki said. "I love my little brother, and I'm sure you'll love yours too."

Pearl shook her head. "I'm talking to my parents as soon as I get home. They're making a terrible mistake!"

# Pearl's News

"MOTHER," PEARL SAID when she arrived home. "Pearl! I'm so glad you're home. Come see what I've done to the baby's room."

Pearl sighed. She didn't want to talk about babies just yet. First, she needed to tell her mother about the festival. "I didn't get to tell you my news yesterday."

Mrs. Swamp put a hand to her mouth. "Oh my goodness. I'm so sorry." She pulled Pearl into their large living room. They sat facing each other on matching gray sea fans.

"Now," Mrs. Swamp said. "Tell me everything."

Pearl couldn't wait any longer. She blurted out, "I am this year's winter princess!"

Pearl's mom squealed with delight. "Oh, how mer-velous! I'm so happy for you."

"It is pretty exciting." Pearl grinned. "Out of all the merkids my name was drawn!"

"You'll be the best winter princess they've ever had!" Mrs. Swamp said. "Did you know that your aunt Joan was a winter princess too?"

"Really?" Pearl said. "I wish she didn't live so far away." Aunt Joan was Pearl's favorite relative, but she lived in the Northern Oceans and they didn't see her often.

"Me too, but maybe she can come to the festival," Mrs. Swamp said. "I will be sure to send her a note today by Black Marlin Express Mail. But first, we need to get you a lovely new dress!"

Now it was Pearl's turn to squeal with excitement. Pearl enjoyed getting new clothes, and shopping with her mother was always fun. They quickly swam to MerLinda's, which had the best dress department in Trident City. While they were looking at clothes, Pearl knew it was time to say something about stinky babies.

"I guess when the baby comes, we won't be able to shop whenever we want," Pearl said slowly.

Her mother looked up from a pretty green gown, but Pearl continued, "We won't be able to go to tea at the Trident Plaza Hotel. Things won't be the same."

Mrs. Swamp hugged Pearl. "Our life will change a bit, but your father and I will always love you. Don't you have more love to share?"

Her mother's arms felt good around

Pearl. Did she really want to share her mother? Pearl frowned before saying, "You might have love to spare, but there's only so much time. Babies take up a lot of time."

"Oh, Pearl, don't worry . . ."

Pearl's mother was interrupted by her father. It was strange to see him in the ladies' department. He looked very much out of place. "Guess what! I've had some wonderful news! Our little fry is arriving early!"

"When?" Pearl asked.

"Tomorrow!" Mr. Swamp said with a big grin.

"How exciting!" Mrs. Swamp squeezed Pearl tightly before hugging her husband.

"Since we're here, shouldn't we do some

shopping for the baby?" Mr. Swamp asked.

"That's a splashing good idea," Mrs. Swamp agreed. "Pearl, why don't you help us pick some things out? We have so much to do!"

Mr. and Mrs. Swamp held hands and floated toward the infants' section of the store. Pearl couldn't believe it. She hadn't gotten her dress, and her mother had forgotten all about her again!

# 5

## Shocked

THE NEXT DAY PEARL TRIED to pay attention to her teacher. "Now, who can tell me a ray that is an active swimmer?" Mrs. Karp asked.

Rocky's hand shot up in the air. "The spotted eagle ray!"

Mrs. Karp smiled. "Right, I can tell you did your homework. Who knows the name of the largest electric ray?"

Pearl looked around the third-grade classroom. No one raised their hand. Pearl hoped Mrs. Karp wouldn't call on her, since she'd forgotten all about the reading assignment. "It makes enough electricity to shock a merperson," Mrs. Karp continued, "and its body is like a big brown sand dollar with a white belly."

Still no one answered. Mrs. Karp sighed. Finally Kiki raised her hand. "Could it be the Atlantic torpedo ray?"

"Yes!" Mrs. Karp said. "Perhaps one of you would like to choose the torpedo ray for your next homework assignment. You are to pretend you are a ray and write a first-person narrative."

Everyone else in the classroom looked just as confused as Pearl felt. "What's a harry tiff?" Rocky asked.

"A first-person narrative," Mrs. Karp explained, "is a story where you pretend to be the main character. I want you to write like you are a ray."

"Any type of ray we want?" Shelly asked.

Mrs. Karp nodded. "You might like to write about the round stingray. We actually have one visiting us today. If you'll be very quiet, she will pass by and let you pet her."

Pearl gulped. Did she dare touch a stingray? She knew its sting could be painful. When the pale ray entered the room and waited gently beside her, she took a chance. "You're so soft," Pearl whispered. The stingray was surprisingly gentle and stopped by every desk.

"Thank you for joining us today," Mrs. Karp said as the stingray floated out of their classroom. "And, merstudents, I'm proud of you for being quiet and calm! Of course, you are all smart enough to never approach a ray by yourself."

Mrs. Karp turned to the doorway. "And now I see Mr. Pebble is here to take you to music class. Since you will be performing at the Winter Festival he has asked for extra practice time with you."

"We do need lots of extra practice,"

Wanda said as they glided into the music room.

Pearl didn't care about music or the festival. Her heart wasn't into playing the drum. She was mad at her mother and father. She was mad at babies. She was even mad at the drum! She banged it as hard as she could.

"Pearl," Mr. Pebble said. "I admire your enthusiasm, but please try to keep time with the other merstudents." He clapped his hands and Pearl beat the drum along with his rhythm.

Every time she hit the drum, Pearl thought about the baby. "Silly baby. Silly baby!" she muttered to herself.

Kiki took her purple fins off her trumpet

fish and nodded at Pearl. "You're pretty good at that."

Pearl smiled for the first time all day. "Thanks. You're the best musician in the whole class."

Kiki smiled back. "My older brother Akeno taught me."

"Your brother?" Pearl asked in surprise.

"Sure, I've learned lots of things from my brothers. My little brother was the one who gave me the idea for the book club."

Mr. Pebble floated beside the mergirls. "Play please."

Pearl banged on the drum again, but she couldn't stop thinking about what Kiki had said. Could she learn from her little brother? Could she teach her little brother something? Pearl laughed to herself. Maybe she could show him how to bang on things!

As they floated down the hall after music class, Wanda tapped Pearl on the arm. "Did you get a new dress yet for the Winter Festival?"

Pearl frowned. Her mother had forgotten about her dress. It was all that baby's fault! With the new baby would her parents even remember that they had a daughter? Suddenly being the winter princess wasn't so exciting anymore.

# Crying Babies and Killer Whales

**C**OME AND MEET YOUR BABY brother! Isn't he adorable?" Mrs. Swamp said when Pearl got home from school.

Pearl squinted at the small fry. He was wrapped tightly in a kelp blanket with only a tiny red face showing. Surprisingly, the little baby looked straight at Pearl with bright-blue eyes and smiled. Pearl grinned back. He was pretty cute.

She didn't smile for long though. Her brother opened his teeny mouth and began squalling. And he didn't stop! The baby merboy cried on and off all evening long. Pearl even heard the little stinker during the night. How could such a small merboy be so loud?

By morning Pearl could barely drag her Venus comb through her hair. At school she was startled when Mrs. Karp asked for her homework.

"Homework?" Pearl asked.

Mrs. Karp nodded. "The narrative story where you pretended to be a ray."

Pearl felt her face turning red. "I-I'm sorry," she stammered. "My new baby brother kept me up half the night. I forgot all about the assignment."

Mrs. Karp's frown changed to a grin. "Oh, I hadn't realized. Congratulations on the new baby. I'm sure he will sleep through the night soon. But do turn in your report tomorrow."

Rocky waved his hand in the air. "Mrs.

Karp, my sea horses are having babies soon. Do I get to skip homework?"

Mrs. Karp didn't answer Rocky, she just shook her head no. All day long Pearl had trouble keeping her eyes open. She yawned when Mrs. Karp told them that rays and sharks don't have bones. She rubbed her eyes when they were supposed to estimate the number of toothlike scales on a common skate. By the end of the day Pearl wasn't even sure if she had the energy to drift home.

Kiki tapped Pearl on the shoulder. "Would you like to stop by my dorm room?"

Pearl nodded. Maybe Kiki would let her rest for a few minutes. Then Pearl remembered that Kiki had a bed made of creepy killer whale bones. Pearl couldn't sit on that! But she was already following Kiki down the watery hall. It would be impolite to swim away now.

Pearl had forgotten how nice Kiki's room was. Rainbow-colored jellyfish lamps hung from the curved ceiling, and a small waterfall tinkled gently in a corner. Glittering plankton covered one wall while a coral reef made another. Everything was shelltacular except the killer whale skeleton bed. Each rib was as big as Pearl's arm. The teeth looked ready to bite her nose! It was as bad as the shark statue at the Trident City Plaza Hotel. She'd always been terrified of it!

"I've been practicing for our performance at the Winter Festival," Kiki said. "Do you want to hear?"

Pearl nodded. She didn't want to be rude, but she really needed to rest. When Kiki played the trumpet fish, Pearl forgot about being tired. She forgot about the Winter Festival. She even forgot about her new baby brother. She just listened to the music and felt peaceful.

The next thing Pearl knew, she woke up in a nest of gray heron feathers inside the skeleton bed. She forgot all about being calm. She was inside a killer whale! She screamed!

# Perfect Dress

**P**EARL RUSHED HOME. SHE couldn't believe she'd fallen asleep inside a killer whale skeleton! And it was all that rotten baby's fault! If she hadn't been so tired, it wouldn't have happened!

She was hungry for an after-school

snack. She hoped someone had made some cuttlefish candy or a coconut shake. Or maybe both! But the kitchen was bare—there wasn't even a crumb on the counter. "I haven't had an afternoon snack all week!" Pearl grumbled. "Do my parents want me to starve to death?"

She found her father and mother huddling over her brother in what used to be the craft room. *Her* craft room! They didn't even notice she was late or that her tummy was rumbling. "Hi, Pearl!" Mrs. Swamp called. "Want to come see the baby?"

"No," Pearl snapped. "I have to do the homework I didn't do last night. I couldn't think with all the crying! I need to get it done before tonight's festival."

As if the baby knew the word, the little squirt began bawling. Pearl twirled her gold tail around and rushed to her room. Even with her door closed, she could hear the wailing. She needed something to keep the noise out. She grabbed the two southern beach moss pillows from her bed. Using her pearl necklace to hold them in place, she covered her ears with them. "Finally," she said. "Peace and quiet."

Pearl sat at her desk and worked on her homework. She jumped when someone tapped her on the shoulder. It was her father. He raised an eyebrow at her pillow ear muffs. "Wwmmm yyyydddrrrrrrnoowww?" he asked.

Pearl pulled the pillows away from her ears. "What?"

"Do you have time to go shopping with me for a winter princess dress?" he asked. "Your mother suggested we go back to MerLinda's."

"Really?" Her father hardly ever took her shopping. Pearl couldn't help being excited. She had planned on wearing her old party dress, even though it was a bit too small.

"Let's go," he said, offering his arm as if they were going to a fancy ball.

Pearl was thrilled to have her father shopping with her at MerLinda's. In fact, when he pulled out a lovely white dress with blue sparkles, she squealed. "Oh, daddy, it's perfect!"

When they got home, Pearl couldn't wait to show it to her mother. She put it on and floated into the living room. Her mother was on their knotted wrack sofa, holding their new baby.

"Pearl, you look lovely!" her mother said. "Even your little brother likes your new dress." Mrs. Swamp guided him to clap his hands.

Pearl giggled. "What is the baby's name?" she asked. "We can't just call him baby for the rest of his life."

"We thought you could help us pick a name," her father said.

"Me?" Pearl said, eager to help. Pearl leaned over the baby and kissed his little head. It was as soft as a stingray and he smelled so sweet!

But what happened next wasn't sweet. It was the most horrible thing ever!

# Slime Time

**H**ER LITTLE BROTHER SPIT green slime all over the front of her beautiful white dress, her face, and even her hair! Pearl was so shocked, she couldn't move.

"Oh no!" her mother shouted.

Her father rushed out of the room and

returned in a mersecond with lots of kelp towels. He blotted the stain, but instead of getting better it spread!

Pearl couldn't believe it. She wanted to sink to the carpet and cry. In fact, that's exactly what she did. "Oh, Pearl, I'm so sorry," her mother told her.

Her father finished dabbing away at the green goop on her face and hair. "See, your hair and face are already back to normal. And we'll get you another dress."

"There isn't time, the store was closing early for the festival," Pearl wailed. She wiped the disgusting front of her dress, trying to clean off the smelly blob. "Instead of being a winter princess, I'm the slime queen!"

*Knock. Knock. Knock.*

"There's someone at the door," her father said. "Let me send them away. Don't worry, we'll figure something out."

Pearl had never felt more miserable or more surprised when four mergirls from her school floated into the room. Kiki, Wanda, Shelly, and Echo were dressed up for the festival and carrying packages wrapped in spectacular seaweed. "Hi, Pearl," her best friend, Wanda, said. "We brought presents for your little brother."

"Be careful, he's dangerous," Pearl warned.

Shelly laughed. "He's only a baby."

"He's a cutie pie!" Echo squealed.

"What's his name?" Kiki asked.

"Trouble with a capital *T*," Pearl muttered. Could her merfriends smell the stinky slime?

"Pearl is only joking. We are still deciding on a name," Mrs. Swamp told them.

"Ooh, I think Edward is a nice name," Shelly suggested.

"How about Figaro?" Wanda asked.

Pearl looked at Wanda like she was crazy. She might not like her little brother, but she wasn't going to name him Figaro!

"What's wrong with Figaro?" Wanda said.

"I've always liked Theodore," Echo said. "There was once a human president named Theodore." Echo loved to learn about humans. Pearl shook her head. She couldn't think about names right now. What was she going to do about the festival? Pearl decided she wouldn't go.

"Alex is a nice name," Kiki whispered. "It means helper."

Pearl jumped up and spread out the bottom of her dress. "He is not a helper. Look what he did!"

Wanda gasped. "Oh no! It's ruined."

"Maybe we can clean it," Shelly suggested.

"We've tried," Pearl said. "It's no use. I'm just not going to the festival!"

"But you're the winter princess," Wanda said.

Pearl slapped her gold tail on the woven Neptune grass carpet. "I'm not going, and there's nothing you can say that will change my mind!"

"There might be one thing," Echo said.

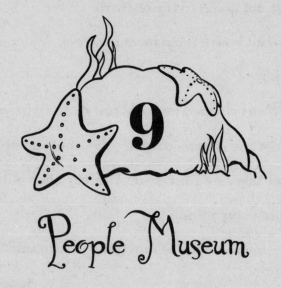

# People Museum

**Y**OU HAVE TO COME WITH US to the People Museum," Echo blurted. "I have an idea."

Pearl shook her head. "I'm going to take a long warm bubble bath and forget I ever heard of the Winter Festival. In fact, I'm never going to go again."

"Pearl, you don't mean that!" Mrs. Swamp said, wiping the baby's mouth.

"Mergirls," Wanda said, "I think we need to talk privately in the hallway."

Pearl rolled her eyes. There was nothing her friends could say to make her change her mind. So she was shocked when just a few minutes later they were pulling her toward the People Museum, the home of the annual Winter Festival. "I can't believe you talked me into this," she muttered.

"Everything is going to be fine," Shelly said.

Kiki nodded. "I have a good feeling."

Pearl looked at her small friend. "Did you have a vision?" Kiki was the only one at Trident Academy who had visions of the future, except for their merology teacher, Madame Hippocampus.

Kiki shook her head. "No, but I still think everything is going to work out."

The mergirls swerved to avoid a silvery catfish as they swam down Museum Lane. "But I don't even have my Venus comb for my hair. It must look horrible after getting spit up on."

"Don't worry," Echo said firmly. "I've read every issue of *MerStyle* magazine. I am going to make you the best winter princess ever."

Normally, Pearl would agree. She'd always thought that she would make a great winter princess, but now she wasn't so sure.

"And we are going to help," Wanda agreed. "We're your beauty team! I learned a lot from your Bubbling Beauty Bunch club."

Pearl groaned. Earlier in the school year she'd formed a beauty club that hadn't gone as well as she'd hoped. Most of the merkids attended just to get free prizes, along with the fresh coconut milk and broiled blobfish burrito snacks.

"And your mom insisted I bring this bag with a Venus comb and other things she packed," Shelly added.

Pearl sighed. It was nice of her mer-friends to help her, but she didn't feel like a princess at all. She felt like a floating disaster!

Echo patted her hand as they glided in a back entrance to the museum. "Listen to me, you have what it takes to be a great winter princess. All you have to do is let us help."

Pearl wiped a dab of baby spit off her pearl necklace. Maybe she could do this. After all, her friends and parents thought she could. Unfortunately, at that moment

they floated past a large mirror that must have come from a sunken ship. Pearl saw her reflection.

A mergirl with a dirty blob on her nose, hair that stuck up in all directions, and a killer-seaweed green stain on her dress stared back from the mirror. It was all Pearl needed to see to make her burst into tears again!

# 10

## The Most Important Thing

**E**VERYONE, UPSTAIRS," SHELLY ordered. She lived with her grandfather in an apartment above the People Museum. He ran the museum with a little help from his granddaughter.

They ushered a still-sobbing Pearl into Shelly's bedroom.

"Can you all get everything we need while I speak to Pearl?" Shelly asked.

Echo, Wanda, and Kiki nodded before dashing out of the room. Shelly handed Pearl some kelp tissues and then began smoothing Pearl's long blond hair with her Venus comb. "Remember when my great-aunt came to tea?" Shelly asked.

Remember? Pearl would never forget the first time she'd met Queen Edwina, Shelly's great-aunt. Pearl had even prepared some delicious treats and told Shelly how to act.

"You helped me then," Shelly continued. "So I want to help you now."

Pearl wiped her eyes. "I'm kind of a mess. Just look at my dress! It's not very princesslike."

Shelly wrinkled her nose at the smell and shrugged. "Queen Edwina told me that the most important thing is for a queen to be honest and help others. I think that applies to princesses too."

Pearl wanted to help the Winter Festival raise shells for the needy. But what about the terrible stain covering the entire front of her dress? What was she going to do? Why did her parents have to adopt a baby this week? Why did they need a baby at all when they had her?

At that instant her merfriends burst

into the room. "Look what we have!" they squealed.

Echo held a white dress that glittered with diamonds.

"I can't wear that," Pearl gasped. "That's the dress from the first Winter Festival." The beautiful gown had hung in the Winter Festival exhibit in the museum for as long as Pearl could remember.

"Oh, yes you can," Wanda said.

Kiki nodded. "Shelly's grandfather said it was fine. After all, this is the twentieth anniversary of the first Winter Festival."

"And," Echo said, with sparkling brown eyes, "it even comes with a crown!"

Pearl couldn't believe it. She was going to get to wear a beautiful crown. This was even better than her original dress. Maybe things would work out after all.

"We'll help you get ready," Shelly said. "The festival starts soon."

"I can't believe you're helping me after I've been so grouchy lately," Pearl said as she slipped her stinky dress off.

"We're your friends," Wanda said.

"You can help me get dressed, on one

condition," Pearl said suddenly. Her mer-friends looked at her in surprise before Pearl grinned. "You all have to be my royal attendants."

Kiki laughed. "It's a deal!"

# Diamond Dress

**P**EARL COULDN'T BELIEVE SHE was actually going to wear the gorgeous diamond dress from the museum. From the first time she'd visited the museum in a shell stroller, she'd loved looking at the sparkles. Now she was going to wear it!

"We'd better hurry," Echo reminded Pearl. "It's only a few minutes before the opening ceremony."

"Okay, let's bubble down and do this!" Pearl said, tossing her stinky dress in a corner.

Pearl giggled as the diamond dress fell over her head. It was surprisingly heavy. Diamonds must weigh a lot! "How does it look?" Pearl asked.

None of her merfriends said a word. They didn't have to. Pearl looked down, and her dream of wearing the diamond dress was crushed. It was too big! It fell off her shoulders, and the bottom puddled around her fins. She'd be lucky to be able to move at all.

"Maybe we can fix it," Kiki said hopefully.

Echo quickly grabbed a handful of the bottom. "We could just cut some of this extra off."

"No wavy way!" Pearl snapped. She couldn't believe Echo had suggested cutting the magnificent museum dress.

"But—" Wanda started to say, before Pearl took a deep breath and surprised herself.

"Give me my stinky dress," Pearl said. "Helping others is what the festival is about, not pretty clothes."

"Wait," Shelly said. "That's not necessary. Your mom sent another dress, but she said it was a little small."

Echo pulled Pearl's old party dress out of her mother's bag. "Oh my Neptune, I'm so glad to see that," Pearl said. Last year's dress would be tight, but at least it wasn't covered with slime!

Pearl squeezed into her old dress, adjusted her pearls, and smoothed her hair. Then she faced her friends and lifted her nose into the water. "Do I look like a winter princess?" she asked.

Wanda shook her head. "No."

"Something is definitely missing." Shelly tapped her chin with the tip of her blue tail.

Pearl shrugged. "Well, I can't help it if my dress isn't perfect, but the show must go on."

Echo grinned and held up the sparkling crown. "This is what you need."

Kiki giggled. "Let's see if it fits."

Pearl held her breath as her merfriends gently set the diamond-studded crown on her head. Was it too big?

"It's shelltacular!" Wanda cheered.

A few minutes later Pearl and her attendants glided into the center of the Grand Hall of the People Museum. White sand had been brought in to cover the floor. Some merkids slid down white slopes while others packed sand together to make pretend mermen and merwomen. Some volunteers even swam overhead to sprinkle white sand. It fell gently to the floor of the museum, sparkling on the way down.

"That's supposed to look like the snow that happens on dry land," Echo whispered.

"It's pretty cool," Pearl said, being careful to keep her head perfectly straight so her lovely crown wouldn't fall off.

"You make a wonderful winter princess," Shelly told her.

"Coming from a real princess, that's a great compliment," Pearl said.

Wanda tapped Pearl on the arm. "Come

on, it's time for you to make your speech."

"Speech?" Pearl gasped. She'd been so concerned about her dress and her new brother that she'd forgotten all about the speech. What was she going to do?

# Good Advice

**P**EARL'S HEART POUNDED AS SHE floated onto the stage in front of hundreds of merfolk. Kiki, Echo, Shelly, and Wanda hovered beside her. The mayor and his son, Rocky, drifted below not far away from her teacher, Mrs. Karp. A few rows back Pearl saw her aunt

Joan beside her parents. Her aunt had come all the way from the Northern Ocean just to see her as winter princess! Her father bounced her little brother up and down in his arms. Pearl remembered he used to do that for her. Her mom put her hands to her mouth and called out, "We love you, Pearl!"

Pearl took a deep breath, looked out over the crowd, and said, "Queen Edwina once said it is important for a queen to be honest and caring. That's good advice for princesses . . ." Pearl paused to smile at Shelly.

"And for us all," Pearl continued. "And I wouldn't be honest if I didn't tell you the truth. I haven't been very caring lately. I thought that how I looked was more important than being kind and helping people. But now I know that's not true. Today, we are all here for a good cause— to help families who need it." Pearl had to pause as the audience clapped.

Pearl looked at her baby brother and her chest felt tight. "I wasn't very caring toward my new baby brother. Especially after he spit up all over me right before the festival." She heard some giggles and gasps.

"Even though families can be messy and sometimes smelly, they can also bring us so much joy," Pearl said firmly. "So this year let's celebrate our families and friends in a special way by sharing hugs and happiness. Let the festival begin!"

All around her merfolk cheered and

hugged one another. Behind her Mr. Pebble tapped his baton for the music to begin. Pearl and her attendants quickly took their places with their instruments. Pearl pounded her drum with a cheerful heart. She even laughed when she saw her father helping her baby brother clap to the beat.

After the song was over, everyone cheered again before moving around the hall to try different activities. Pearl swam over to her family and hugged each one, even her little brother. She patted his soft head. "Since he's as soft as a stingray, what if we named him Ray?" Pearl suggested.

Pearl's aunt Joan chuckled. "Ray means king, so you'll be the princess and he'll be the little king, or prince."

Pearl's mother smiled. "Ray is perfect, just like our family!"

Pearl hugged Ray again. He grabbed her pearl necklace and began sucking on it.

"No, no." Pearl's father told the baby. "Don't get slobber on Pearl's necklace."

Pearl laughed. "Oh, I don't mind," she said. And the funny thing was, she meant it!

# Class Reports

★ ✦ ★

**BLUE-SPOTTED STINGRAY**

*by Shelly Siren*

Just call me Bobbi Jo. I'm a stingray!

That's right, I'm not one of those wimpy

rays that can't sting someone who bothers

me. You grab me and I'll whip

my blue-striped tail at

you faster than you

can say "Ouch!"

## MANTA RAY

by Echo Reef

Let me tell you this.

It is not nice to call

anyone names. After

all, I'm a nice peaceful ray. I don't bother

anyone. In fact, I've even danced with

humans and merfolk a few times. But does

that stop people from calling me names

like "devil ray"? Nope, but I tell you it's

not fair. Just because I have these hornlike

lobes, people resort to name-calling. It's

not right!

## SMALLTOOTH SAWFISH

by Rocky Ridge

I bet you wish you had a snout like mine!

I'm pretty proud of it. I use my long flat rostrum to dig for shellfish. Yum! There's nothing like a nice crunchy crab.

### RETICULATE WHIPRAY
by Kiki Coral

My favorite thing to do is float quietly in sandy patches between rocks, near the shore. Everyone thinks I just like the warm water, but the real reason is that I

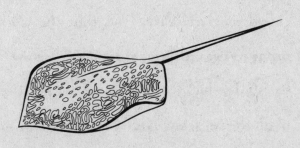

like to watch people. If you've ever seen a human, you know how strange they are. They see me and start saying things like, "It's diamond-shaped!" and "Look at its pointed snout!" Don't they think I know what I look like? Why do they need to tell me? Like I said, people are weird!

## PAINTED RAY

by Pearl Swamp

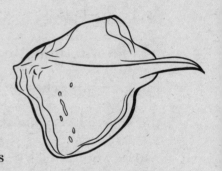

My friends call me Paint, but in school my teachers called me Undulate. Isn't that the worst name ever? Although I guess Figaro is worse. I'm lucky to be one of the prettiest of all the rays, but even luckier because the pattern on my wings helps me to hide from humans. They think I look pretty in their aquariums, but I like the bottom of the sea much better!

# The Mermaid Song Tales

**REFRAIN:**

*Let the water roar*

*Deep down we're swimming along*

*Twirling, swirling, singing the mermaid song.*


**VERSE 1:**

*Shelly flips her tail*

*Racing, diving, chasing a whale*

*Twirling, swirling, singing the mermaid song.*

**VERSE 2:**

*Pearl likes to shine*

*Oh my Neptune, she looks so fine*

*Twirling, swirling, singing the mermaid song.*


**VERSE 3:**

*Shining Echo flips her tail*

*Backward and forward without fail*

*Twirling, swirling, singing the mermaid song.*


**VERSE 4:**

*Amazing Kiki*

*Far from home and floating so free*

*Twirling, swirling, singing the mermaid song.*

# Author's Note

FAMILIES COME IN ALL SIZES. I have two brothers and we didn't always get along when we were kids. I have two sons and a daughter who didn't always get along either! It is actually normal for brothers and sisters to have arguments from time to time.

Many famous people were adopted. If you've ever eaten at a restaurant named Wendy's, you might know that the founder,

Dave Thomas, was adopted as a baby. Steve Jobs, the cofounder of Apple, Inc. (which makes iPads and iPhones), was adopted at birth. I am very lucky that one of my children came to our family through adoption. He made our family complete.

Your friend,

Debbie Dadey

# Glossary

**ATLANTIC GUITARFISH:** This ray uses its spineless tail for swimming, like a shark.

**ALTANTIC TORPEDO RAY:** This ray is the largest electric ray. Electricity is stored in the ray's wings, which it uses to stun its prey.

**BANJO RAY:** Also known as a fiddler ray, the banjo ray lives along the coasts of Australia.

**BLACK DRUM:** This fish is a bottom dweller. It actually makes a bongo drumbeat sound when searching for a mate.

**BLACK MARLIN:** The black marlin is one of the fastest fish on the planet. The female usually weighs hundreds of pounds more than the male.

**BLOBFISH:** Living in deep waters off Australia, this fish truly does look like a blob!

**CATFISH:** The gafftopsail sea catfish lives in the Atlantic Ocean and has very long whiskerlike barbels.

**COCONUT:** Coconuts are a fruit that's hard on the outside, but the inside is part solid and part milk.

**CORAL:** Coral reefs may not look alive, but the multicolored skeleton is made by small saclike animals. One quarter of all ocean species depend on reefs for food and shelter.

**CORNETFISH**: This long, skinny fish is related to the sea horse.

**COMMON SKATE**: Also called the blue skate because of its bluish underside, the common skate is the largest and heaviest of the European rays. It is extinct in some areas.

**CONCH**: The spiral shell of this mollusk is sometimes used as a horn.

**CUTTLEFISH**: The giant cuttlefish can actually change color.

**FRY**: Baby fish are referred to as fry.

**GLASS SQUID**: This mollusk has light organs in its arms and eyes. It is also known as the transparent cockatoo squid.

**KILLER SEAWEED**: This is actually a type of seaweed that is used in marine aquariums. It grows quickly on the seabed and is toxic to grazers.

**GRAY HERON:** The gray heron is the largest heron in Europe. It has a long neck, long yellow legs, and a pointed bill. It is often photographed for its beauty.

**KELP:** Giant kelp is the largest seaweed.

**KILLER WHALE:** The killer whale is the largest dolphin. Also called an orca, it is easily recognized by its black-and-white markings.

**KNOTTED WRACK:** This brown seaweed can be found on rocky seashores in cooler climates. In the summertime it may turn yellow.

**MAUVE STINGER JELLYFISH:** This jellyfish can put on beautiful light shows, but don't get too close, because its stingers hurt!

**MOTHER-OF-PEARL:** Some mollusks make a coating for the inside of their shells. This mother-of-pearl, or nacre, protects the mollusks. In the past the nacre was used to make jewelry.

**NEPTUNE GRASS:** Neptune grass is also known as Mediterranean tapeweed. Neptune grass beds can be thousands of years old.

**PLANKTON:** These small creatures cannot swim. They float freely in the ocean. They are the main food source for many large ocean creatures, including whales.

**PEARL:** Beadlike pearls are formed in oysters when a grain of sand irritates the inside of their shells. They coat the sand with nacre, forming pearls.

**ROUND STINGRAY:** This circular-shaped ray lives off the western shore of the United States and has a painful sting.

**SAND DOLLAR:** When dead, sand dollars are white with a five-pointed shape on their back. Dark purple spines cover the star design on living sand dollars.

**SEA HORSE:** The sea horse belongs to a genus of fish called Hippocampus. The Ancient Greek word *hippos* means horse and the word *kampos* means sea monster.

**SEA SLUG:** Sea slugs have an amazing sense of smell which they can use to locate food in a maze.

**SHARK:** There are more than four hundred types of sharks. While some people think sharks are bad, they are actually important in regulating the fish population.

**SPECTACULAR SEAWEED:** This colorful seaweed grows in deep waters.

**SPOTTED EAGLE RAY:** The pattern of spots on this ray's back (dorsal surface) makes it one of the prettiest rays. It can make spectacular leaps out of the water.

**SOUTHERN BEACH MOSS:** This moss grows on coastal rocks.

**TRUMPET FISH:** This long thin fish has a mouth that looks like the mouthpiece on a trumpet. While Kiki is able to make music with a trumpet fish, in the wild they are very quiet.

**VENUS COMB:** The shell of this sea snail looks like a spiky comb.

# Debbie Dadey

is an award-winning children's book author who has written more than 160 books. She is best known for her series the Adventures of the Bailey School Kids, written with Marcia Thornton Jones. Debbie lives with her husband and two dogs in Sevierville, Tennessee. She is not a mermaid . . . yet.

# The Secret Rescuers

**EBOOK EDITIONS ALSO AVAILABLE**
From Aladdin
simonandschuster.com/kids

# Candy Fairies

Chocolate Dreams

Rainbow Swirl

Caramel Moon

Cool Mint

Magic Hearts

Gooey Goblins

The Sugar Ball

A Valentine's Surprise

Bubble Gum Rescue

Double Dip

Jelly Bean Jumble

The Chocolate Rose

A Royal Wedding

Marshmallow Mystery

Frozen Treats

The Sugar Cup

Sweet Secrets

Taffy Trouble

The Coconut Clue

Rock Candy Treasure

A Minty Mess

The Peppermint Princess

Mini Sweets

## Visit candyfairies.com for games, recipes, and more!

**EBOOK EDITIONS ALSO AVAILABLE**
FROM ALADDIN • SIMONANDSCHUSTER.COM/KIDS

# Solve each problem with the smartest third-grade inventor!

FRANKIE SPARKS, THIRD-GRADE INVENTOR

FRANKIE SPARKS AND THE CLASS PET
BOOK 1

BY MEGAN FRAZER BLAKEMORE ILLUSTRATED BY NADJA SARELL

FRANKIE SPARKS, THIRD-GRADE INVENTOR

FRANKIE SPARKS AND THE TALENT SHOW TRICK
BOOK 2

BY MEGAN FRAZER BLAKEMORE ILLUSTRATED BY NADJA SARELL

FRANKIE SPARKS, THIRD-GRADE INVENTOR

FRANKIE SPARKS AND THE BIG SLED CHALLENGE
BOOK 3

BY MEGAN FRAZER BLAKEMORE ILLUSTRATED BY NADJA SARELL

FRANKIE SPARKS, THIRD-GRADE INVENTOR

FRANKIE SPARKS AND THE LUCKY CHARM
BOOK 4

BY MEGAN FRAZER BLAKEMORE ILLUSTRATED BY NADJA SARELL

EBOOK EDITIONS ALSO AVAILABLE

Aladdin
simonandschuster.com/kids

# Making friends one Sparkly nail at a time!

# Nancy Drew
## ✶ CLUE BOOK ✶

Nancy Drew · CLUE BOOK · Pool Party Puzzler
by CAROLYN KEENE · illustrated by PETER FRANCIS

Nancy Drew · CLUE BOOK · 2 · Last Lemonade Standing
by CAROLYN KEENE · illustrated by PETER FRANCIS

Nancy Drew · CLUE BOOK · 3 · A Star Witness
by CAROLYN KEENE · illustrated by PETER FRANCIS

Nancy Drew · CLUE BOOK · 4 · Big Top Flop
by CAROLYN KEENE · illustrated by PETER FRANCIS

Nancy Drew · CLUE BOOK · 5 · Movie Madness
by CAROLYN KEENE · illustrated by PETER FRANCIS

Nancy Drew · CLUE BOOK · 6 · Pets on Parade
by CAROLYN KEENE · illustrated by PETER FRANCIS

Nancy Drew · CLUE BOOK · 7 · Candy Kingdom Chaos
by CAROLYN KEENE · illustrated by PETER FRANCIS

Nancy Drew · CLUE BOOK · 8 · World Record Mystery
by CAROLYN KEENE · illustrated by PETER FRANCIS

Nancy Drew · CLUE BOOK · 9 · Springtime Crime
by CAROLYN KEENE · illustrated by PETER FRANCIS

Nancy Drew · CLUE BOOK · 10 · Zoo Crew
by CAROLYN KEENE · illustrated by PETER FRANCIS

Nancy Drew · CLUE BOOK · The Tortoise and the Scare
by CAROLYN KEENE · illustrated by PETER FRANCIS

Test your detective skills with Nancy and her best friends, Bess and George!

**NancyDrew.com**

## EBOOK EDITIONS ALSO AVAILABLE
From Aladdin ✶ simonandschuster.com/kids

Looking for another great book?
Find it
**IN THE MIDDLE**.

Fun, fantastic books for kids
in the in-be**TWEEN** age.

IntheMiddleBooks.com

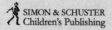